ZOM[ ]

D0376553

Evan Jacobs

SADDLEBACK
EDUCATIONAL PUBLISHING

red rhino
b OO k s™

Clan Castle	Racer
The Code	Sky Watchers
The Garden Troll	Stolen Treasure
The Gift	The Soldier
I Am Underdog	**Zombies!**
The Lost House	Zuze and the Star

With more titles on the way …

SADDLEBACK
EDUCATIONAL PUBLISHING
www.sdlback.com

ISBN-13: 978-1-62250-896-9
ISBN-10: 1-62250-896-3
eBook: 978-1-63078-028-9

Printed in Guangzhou, China
NOR/0714/CA21401177

18 17 16 15 14   1 2 3 4 5

LEO the LIAR

Age: 10

Most Crazy Lie: that his brother is from Mars

First Halloween Costume: Pinocchio

Favorite Ice Cream: raspberry ripple—
it looks like blood

Best Quality: wants to be a good person

LAMEBRAIN the ZOMBIE

Age: 103

Current Goal: to keep the rest of his tongue

Best Friend: the maggot that lives in his pinky toe

Favorite Food: food, what's that?

Best Quality: doesn't need any sleep

1
LEO THE LIAR

"Then," Leo Jennings said. "I saw zombies walk down the street. I had to hide behind a big car." He smiled. "I didn't want to be seen."

Leo was telling a story. Like always. He was known all over school for telling stories. Recess was almost over. Soon, all the kids would go back to class.

Two students sat in front of Leo. They were brothers. They were new in school. They didn't know Leo. That he loved scary movies. That he loved to tell stories. That he was known as "Leo the Liar."

LEO the LIAR !!

Leo didn't mind that name. He always had stories to tell. He didn't think they were lies. He thought they were cool. Like the time he saved a family from a fire. Or when he fell from a six-story building. And lived.

None of it ever happened. But Leo didn't care. He just made up more.

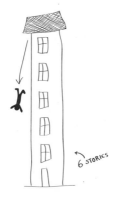

6 STORIES

Leo was about to tell the new kids how he saved the town. He tried to stop himself. It was hard. He had so many stories to tell. He had seen many scary movies. Leo had a lot in his head. A story came into his mind. He had to tell it.

This story was scary. Leo was out late. He saw something. His town was filled with zombies. A loud voice broke into his head.

"Leo the Liar. You telling lies again?" Adam Ortiz. He didn't like Leo.

Leo saw Adam. He was standing with Manuel Mendez. And Angelo Setari.

3

"No." Leo swallowed hard. He knew Adam would not believe him. "I was just telling …"

Leo turned. He saw the two brothers. They had walked away. As soon as they could. He was sad. At first. But Leo knew he did that to people.

"Another big lie," Adam said.

Adam moved closer to Leo. Manuel and Angelo moved in.

"The bell is about to ring," Leo said. He eyed his watch. "Why not wait till lunch? You'll have a whole forty minutes to get me."

"Forty minutes!" Adam laughed.

Manuel and Angelo smiled.

"I'm just gonna need four seconds. I told you to stop your lies. You didn't. Now you're gonna pay."

Adam grabbed Leo by the shirt. He held up his fist. Leo closed his eyes.

He was going to get pounded. And he didn't want to see it.

← KNUCKLE
SANDWICH

"Your mouth! It will get you in trouble one day." That's what his parents always said. And now look.

2
THE PROOF

Then Leo had an idea.

"Wait!" he yelled. Adam let him go. "I can get proof. I'll show you. There are zombies. Zombies all over this town!"

THEY ARE EVEN AT THE MOVIES!

More students had come around. They all wanted to see. Leo was going to get what he deserved. He knew it. One day he was going to have to pay for his lies.

Is this it? he thought. *Will Adam buy it?*

"Let's see your proof," Adam said.

"I can get it." Leo was feeling it. He needed to talk. To tell a story. Stories got him excited. Once he started talking, his idea would grow. It was like he *needed* to tell stories. It made him feel good. "I'm gonna get you proof. Pictures of zombies walking around late at night."

"How?" asked Adam.

"Don't worry about it," Leo snapped.

Many students gasped.

Adam Ortiz! He was the toughest kid in school. Leo was only a fourth grader. No one had ever stood up to Adam like this. He was in sixth grade.

"Bring it Monday," Adam said. He pushed his finger into Leo's chest. "And they'd better be real. Or else. I wouldn't come to school ever again."

"And what happens when I bring it?" Leo asked.

"I guess you won't be Leo the Liar anymore. Right, Leo the Liar?"

"I'll come with proof. Then you can't call me that. Ever again. Nobody can. And if they do? Well, you have to stop them."

"Or what?"

"I know zombies. I'm friends with them,"

Leo lied. "Do you really want to mess with me? A kid who is friends with zombies."

"Just bring your proof." Adam walked away. Manuel and Angelo followed. "We'll deal with it Monday."

Leo looked at the other kids. They were staring at him. Then they walked away.

After lunch Leo couldn't concentrate. Mrs. Moore was talking science. Nobody would look at Leo. It was like he was sick. If they looked at him, they would get sick too. Leo Jennings knew he was in trouble. He had told one lie too many. He had been warned.

MIXING

CHEMICALS

I CAN'T CONCENTRATE!

"Your mouth will get you in trouble one day." He heard his parents' words again.

And he was in for it. He just didn't know how much.

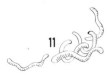

3
SNEAKING OUT

Leo was very good when he got home. He didn't want any attention. He had to sneak out later. He didn't want to get caught. He needed a plan to get "proof."

Adam, Manuel, and Angelo acted tough. But they didn't go out late at night. Leo didn't either. But he was going out late tonight. He had to get his "zombies."

He was going to use his phone's camera. It didn't take good pictures. And it would be dark. Hard to see. So Leo would shoot shadows. People walking outside. Animals. Anything out at night. "Those aren't zombies!" He could hear it now. Adam would know.

"Yes, they are," Leo would say. He knew he couldn't get a real zombie photo. But no way could Adam prove it.

After dinner Leo watched movies. To get in the monster mood. He watched *ParaNorman* and *Monster House*. He liked those movies a lot.

Leo had seen lots of scary movies. None of them really scared him. Still, he held out hope. He liked to be scared. He wanted to be scared.

He loved *Fangoria*. It was a magazine. He used pictures from the magazine for his room. They covered the walls. His bookshelf was filled with scary books.

At 9:45 p.m. it was lights out. Almost every night. His parents let him watch movies till ten. But only on Friday and Saturday. They put his six-year-old brother,

Arnold, to bed earlier. Then his parents went to sleep.

By midnight everyone would be zonked. Leo would just be getting started.

He set the alarm on his phone. Then closed his eyes. He had to be awake in two hours.

Beep. Beep. Beep.

Leo looked at his phone. 12:03 a.m.

He was still wearing his clothes. He wanted to be ready fast. He put his phone in his pocket. Then he gently opened the door. And peered out. The upstairs hallway was clear. The door to his parents' bedroom was shut. So was the door to Arnold's room.

"Perfect," he whispered.

Leo went quietly down the hall. To the stairs. Then down to the front door. He held his breath. Turned the knob. Then slowly pulled the door open. It was cold outside. He felt the chill on his cheek. So far everything was quiet.

He tiptoed outside. Then gently shut the door. He walked quietly down the porch steps. He felt bad not locking the door. He couldn't. It would make too much noise. Leo couldn't take the chance. He needed everyone to stay asleep.

UNLOCKED

He was having fun. But soon the thrill wore off. Real life hit him like a ton of bricks.

First, it was cold! He forgot a hoodie. He left his house so fast. *Brrr!* Second, it was too dark for pictures. They looked black. Nobody would be fooled. Third, Leo knew there were no zombies. Zombies were not real.

1ˢᵗ BRRR

2ᴺᴰ ZOMBIE 1 ZOMBIE 2 ZOMBIE 3 TOO DARK

3ᴿᴰ ← DON'T EXIST!

Why did I say I would get proof? he thought. *Zombies don't even exist!*

Out of nowhere an old yellow cab pulled up. Its engine made all kinds of sounds.

Ticking. Creaking. Groaning. Its yellow paint was faded. There were dents. Dings. Cracks. And the right taillight was smashed.

WHERE DID THIS HUNK-O-JUNK COME FROM?

TAXI

Leo put his hand in his pocket. He had five dollars. It was lunch money he'd saved. He did that sometimes. He liked to buy candy. Or scary DVDs from the store.

Leo couldn't see the driver. He heard the window being rolled down.

"Need a ride?" The driver's voice was deep. And scratchy.

"Will five dollars get me across town? It's a ten-minute walk." Leo held up his money.

"That's more than enough," the driver said.

He pressed a button. The back door opened.

Leo got inside. The cab drove away.

The seats were dirty. Torn up. But something else bothered Leo. The smell. It was bad. It smelled like something had died. And it was rotting. Yep. Something was dead.

"Having a little fun, are we?" the driver asked. "You're outside. You should be asleep."

"Yeah." Leo didn't really want to talk. He blinked. Did something just fall off the driver's face? Nah. It was too dark to see much.

"Does the night scare you?" the driver asked. "Don't worry. The morning light will be here soon." The cab came to a stop sign. The driver turned on an inside light. Leo's mouth dropped. Oh no!

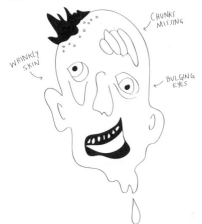

The driver's skin was wrinkled. Some chunks dripped off his face. Other chunks clung. His eyes were bulging. Bloodshot. His veins looked like they were about to pop.

And that thing Leo saw fall from the driver's face? A worm! Worms! Worms squirmed out of the driver's ear. Gross!

"You're a-a ..." Leo stuttered.

"Zombie?" The driver smiled. Then he pressed the gas pedal down.

Leo quickly opened the door. He leaped onto the street. Rolled. Then somehow landed on his feet. He started running. The cab did a U-turn. It was coming back for him.

4
HELP?

Leo dashed across a large park. Over a bridge. And into another neighborhood. By now he was breathless. But he knew he had to keep running.

He rounded a corner. He saw the lights from the cab. It was turning in his direction. Leo quickly jumped into some bushes.

"Ah!" he cried. The tall bushes were prickly. Within seconds, Leo started to itch.

The longer he hid, the worse it would be. He knew that.

The cab slowly went down the street. It was as if the driver knew. He knew he was torturing Leo.

It took forever. But the cab passed him. Leo waited even longer. He wanted to make sure it was gone. Long gone.

WAITING FOR ZOMBIE CAB TO DISAPPEAR

Leo started running again. He came to another street. He couldn't believe his luck. There was a cop. He was sitting on his motorcycle. Wearing a helmet. Visor pulled down.

Leo was going to get it. He just knew. If he went over to the cop, he was going to be in trouble. He was out way too late for a kid. Trouble was coming.

"I don't care!" he told himself. "Anything is better than being chased by that zombie." So he took a deep breath. "Officer!" Leo yelled. Just like he'd been taught to do when he was in danger. "There's a man. There's a zombie driving a yellow cab!"

"What?" the officer asked. "Did you say 'zombie'?"

The cop flipped up his visor.

Leo wanted to barf.

The cop's face was half bone. A skeleton, really. Rotting skin covered the other half. The bone was brown and chipped. The officer's face was yellow and sagging.

"Ahh!" Leo yelled as he ran down the street.

Then he stopped. He could not run another step.

And not because he was tired.

In the distance was a mob of zombies.

Maybe a hundred! They walked in a slow and steady way. Just like in the movies.

And they were coming right at Leo.

5

THE TRUTH

There was one option. And only one. Leo knew it.

He ran to the first house he saw. The sign above the door read The Ramirez Family. Leo banged on the door. He needed help. Yeah, it was nighttime. But he was alone. And scared. He banged again. As hard as he could. Within seconds a light went on in the front room.

Leo breathed a big sigh of relief.

The door opened.

A man stood there. He looked angry. His wife was behind him. And so were his two kids. Leo knew them from school. Their names were Mia and Marina.

"What do you want?" Mr. Ramirez growled.

"There are zombies out here!" Leo turned and pointed at the street. "Look!"

Leo's jaw dropped. He could not believe it. The zombies were gone. The street was empty.

Where was the zombie cop? He was gone too.

"What the heck?" Leo said.

"That's Leo. He's in Mrs. Moore's class," Marina said. "He's always telling lies. Then he gets in trouble."

MARINA IS A TATTLETALE

"I'm not lying!" Leo yelled. "There are zombies all over town. I know you don't see them now. But they really are everywhere!"

"Do your parents know you're out?" Mrs. Ramirez asked. "It's so late!"

"I should call the police," Mr. Ramirez said.

"Call them," Leo said. "We're gonna need

help. All we can get. The town is gonna become Zombieland if we don't get help!"

Mr. Ramirez started to shut the door.

"Go home. Get some sleep. Or you're gonna be in big trouble," Mr. Ramirez said.

Leo stuck his leg in the door. He didn't want to get shut out. "Can I at least come inside?" He held up his phone. "I'll call my parents! I just want to get off the—"

But Mr. Ramirez gave him a shove. And before Leo could say another word, the door was slammed shut.

The lights went off in the house. And Leo was alone again.

6

LONG WALK HOME

He was afraid. He had to walk home. He'd never been on this side of town. He had to face facts. He was lost. Was he going the right way?

"Hey, boy," a familiar voice called. "Wanna lift?"

It was the zombie cabbie. He was only feet away.

Leo looked at him. A streetlight shone on his cab. The driver smiled his crooked smile. Most of his zombie teeth had rotted out. A hunk of skin fell off his face. Some worms crawled out of his nose.

FROM HIS NOSE!

Leo felt himself starting to get sick. He didn't have time for this. He had to run. If he didn't, the zombie cabdriver would get him. That was for sure.

Leo tore off down the street. The cab followed.

Leo ran over lawns. Hopped over flowers. He did all he could to get away from the crazy zombie.

"Help! Help! A zombie is trying to kill me!" Leo yelled.

There was nobody on the street to hear him. Cars were parked in front of every house. None of the lights came on. Nobody came outside.

Can't they hear me? Leo wondered. *Why aren't they helping? Is it because I always tell stories?*

Leo continued to scream. He yelled at the top of his lungs.

Somebody had to be up. Somebody had to hear him.

Nothing.

Leo felt his lungs starting to burn.

His legs were getting heavier with every step.

Leo was getting tired. How much longer could he run? He didn't know. He heard the zombie cabdriver laugh. It was low at first. But it seemed to be getting louder. And louder.

ZOMBIE LAUGH

He tried to run faster. Leo turned corners. Stomped down a sidewalk. Passed street sign after street sign. But his house was no closer.

"Somebody! Anybody! Please help me!"
He was panting. He could barely get the
words out. "I won't lie anymore. I promise!"

And then he rounded a corner. It was his
block! His prayers had been answered. His
house was there. At the end of the street.
Leo slowed down. Just a little.

The zombie cab rounded the corner.

Leo got excited. He turned. Looked at the
zombie.

A ZOMBIE
MUST HAVE
DROPPED THIS

"Keep coming, zombie guy!" Leo laughed.
"My dad is going to get you. My neighbors
are going to get you. You won't win."

Then Leo ran faster. He didn't want to
get caught.

He was close to his house. Twenty yards. Then he noticed something.

There were people outside. Blocking his house.

Did they find out about the zombies? Leo wondered. *Are they here to help?*

Leo realized he hadn't taken pictures. It had been too crazy. But that was fine. These people would say he was telling the truth. They would say they saw zombies too.

Adam, Angelo, and Manuel would have the proof they wanted.

Leo was almost home.

"Hey!" he yelled. "The zombie cab is behind me. Get him!"

The people didn't respond. They didn't do anything.

That's because they were not people.

They were zombies.

And they were on Leo's front lawn. They were moving toward his house!

7

AIM FOR THE HEAD

"No!" Leo yelled.

Again, nobody heard him.

He ran toward his house. He had no idea what he was going to do. Then he saw something. Over there! Leo saw a bike. And a baseball bat. Both were in the grass.

JEFF AND JOHN BANKS ARE CARELESS WITH THEIR TOYS

They belonged to Jeff and John Banks. They used to play with Leo. But he told too many lies. So they stopped. It was like that with every kid. In the neighborhood. At school. Nobody played with a liar.

Leo never really cared before. He had his scary movies. His computer. His iPad. And his mind. That was all he needed.

ALL I NEED!

But now? He could've used some friends.

Leo ran over. Grabbed the bat. And hopped on the bike.

He was scared. At first.

What if the Banks brothers got mad? He was using their stuff. Leo knew he didn't have another choice.

"I have to save my family," he said.

Leo eyed the zombie gang.

They were slow. They hadn't gotten to the porch. Leo got a sinking feeling in his stomach. Yikes! The front door was unlocked!

Leo had been so worried about his lie. He had been so focused on getting the photos. He didn't lock the door. All because he didn't want to get caught. The lock was loud. He would be busted when he came home. For sure. So he'd left it unlocked.

Leo was thinking about himself. Now it had come back to haunt him.

He had to save his family. He started to peddle fast. Leo lifted the bat.

"Ahh!" he yelled.

Leo rode in front of the first zombie wave. The ones closest to the front door. Leo hit each in the head. He did his best to keep moving.

There was only one problem. The grass was wet. And muddy. It wasn't easy.

Zombies grabbed for him. Their rotten hands ran over his shirt. Through his hair. On his skin. Yuck!

Leo had seen many horror movies. Most of them were gross. Filled with blood. He loved them all. These zombies were different. They didn't look cool. They were gross. Eyes hanging. Teeth dangling. Open sores. Blood and brains dripping. These zombies were moving slow. But they didn't stop.

Even the ones Leo had smashed stood up again.

Leo swung the bat hard. He hit some. He didn't hit others. But he kept swinging. He was at the front door. They were so close. The bike was no good. Where could he go?

EYEBALLS FLYING

He had to fight back. For himself. For his brother. For his parents. They moved closer. And closer. Leo tried to get away. But he couldn't. The zombies were everywhere. Leo couldn't move.

Now he could smell them. They smelled worse than trash. The smell was getting stronger. Leo couldn't breathe!

They had him now.

8
LIGHT

The zombies' arms grabbed him. Just like Leo had seen in scary movies.

He was pressed up against the door now. He couldn't swing the bat. Leo wanted to go inside. But he knew that was the wrong move. They would find a way in. They always did. Leo had to remain strong. He had to protect his family. No matter what.

Whoa. There was a bright light. And it was coming from behind the zombies. The light was blinding. He could see them now. There were so many. They were all over the lawn. And the sidewalk.

Leo closed his eyes. The zombies were going to get him. He didn't want to see it.

Any moment now. Any moment. He would feel their creepy hands on his face. It wouldn't take long. Then Leo would be one of them.

GET THOSE CREEPY HANDS AWAY!

Nothing happened.

Leo opened his eyes. The light was even brighter. But the zombies had backed off. They were still feet away. But they had been *inches* away.

Even stranger? The swarm had parted. Right down the middle. The path led to the light.

RIGHT DOWN THE MIDDLE

Leo didn't know what was happening. The zombies had been stopped. He knew they didn't like fire. Was the light like fire? Was it scaring the zombies?

Leo grabbed the bike. He peddled

through the opening. Whoever was at the end? That person was a lifesaver.

He peddled by. He watched the zombies. They were moving in place. Like a dance.

ZOMBIE DANCE

Leo turned toward the light again. It got brighter. Leo could see a person smiling at him. Then he saw that there were two people. Who could they be?

Leo crashed! *Splat*! He landed on the hard street. He couldn't believe it.

The people? They weren't human at all.

It was the zombie cabdriver. And the zombie cop. They were shining the lights.

Leo jumped to his feet. Both zombies grinned at him.

"Why did you help me?" Leo cried.

"We didn't help you," said the zombie cabdriver.

"No! We didn't help you." The zombie cop was laughing. Leo didn't get it. What was the joke?

"We helped them!" They pointed at the front door.

Leo's heart sank.

The zombies were at the front door. The unlocked door. And it was Leo's fault. They opened it. Now they were going inside!

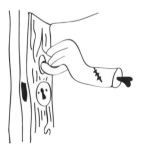

9

FAMILY COMES FIRST

Leo ran back. He had to beat off the monsters. He swung the bat. Hard! *Smack*! Contact! Zombie after zombie fell. Leo couldn't get into his house fast enough.

ZOMBIE GUTS

The zombies began to swarm him again!

They were too close to hit. Leo fell to the ground. He crawled between rotting legs. He was still holding the bat. It seemed useless. There were so many zombies.

Leo crawled fast. Then he was back in his house.

He wanted to shut the door. But there were too many zombies inside. They were in the living room. The kitchen. Some started up the stairs.

"Get out! Now!" Leo began hitting monsters. *Smack*! *Smack*! *Thump*! The bat made contact. Again. And again. Zombies dropped to the floor. Sometimes Leo missed. He'd hit a picture. Or a plant.

MOM IS GOING TO BE MAD!

Soon, Leo made his way to the stairs. Another zombie. *Smack*! He bashed it.

He had to get to the top. To his parents'

room. To his brother. To save his family. He turned. He faced the zombies again.

This batch was gross. Worse than the last. Yellow puss. Green puss. Oozing puss. Sick. Their skin flaked off. They looked … crumbly. Like they would break apart.

One zombie opened its mouth. Maggots poured out.

TALK ABOUT MAGGOT BREATH

Another one had half a face.

Leo swung the bat. Hard! *Smack*! *Thwack*! He knocked down a lot of monsters.

He saw the front door. There were so many. They kept coming.

SMACK!! THWACK!

Leo hit even more. Then he turned. He ran up the stairs. His home used to be safe. Now it wasn't. Because of him. It was a nightmare. For real.

Finally he was upstairs. A zombie was close to his parents' door. Leo had to be fast. Or the monster would get there first.

There were no door locks. They were taken off long ago. Leo was little. Arnold was a baby. They locked themselves in a bathroom. The lock broke. They were trapped. Their mom freaked out. So their dad changed all the knobs. *Poof*! No more locks.

Leo held up the bat. He tried to throw it. Like a missile.

The bat didn't move. Huh?

Leo spun around. A zombie held it. Leo would have to fight for it.

"Hey!" Leo screamed.

He kicked the zombie. Hard in the leg. Bone dust exploded. The zombie's leg broke in two. The monster fell to the floor.

IT FELL RIGHT OFF!

"That's what you get for messing with my family!"

Leo picked up the bat. He turned around. And threw it.

The zombie had his hand on his parents'

doorknob. He was just turning it. When *bam*! The bat hit him in the head. The head went flying. The monster fell to the ground.

Still the zombies kept coming. Louder and louder. There were so many.

Leo ran over to his parents' room. He picked up the baseball bat. Then he went inside.

The light was on.

There they were. His mom. His dad. Arnold. They were all in their pajamas. They didn't look scared. They looked mad. Arnold was crying.

"What are you doing?" his dad asked.

"I'm—" Leo started.

"Why are you throwing things?" his mom asked.

"Your brother ran in here. Said you were acting crazy." His dad was calm. Arnold cried easily. He didn't want him more wound up.

"But there were …" Leo said.

He ran over to the bedroom window. There was a bright light. Leo looked. The light was coming from a street lamp.

NO ZOMBIES?

There were no zombies outside. The cabdriver? Gone. The cop? Gone too. What? Where did they go?

"There were zombies here. They were outside. They were inside. They were everywhere!" Leo's voice cracked. Now he regretted not taking any pictures.

Leo left their room. He ran over to the stairs. There were no zombies inside either. The front door was shut. And locked.

"Leo! You are grounded this weekend," his dad said.

Leo turned and saw his family. They were staring.

What was going on?

10

LESSON LEARNED

That night changed Leo. The weekend was not normal. It was different.

Leo didn't stay inside. He didn't play on the computer. He didn't stay up late watching scary movies.

He went outside. He played with the Banks brothers. He played with other kids too.

He didn't tell any stories.

He didn't get zombie pictures. But Leo stopped being mad at himself. It was too dark. And he was too scared to take pictures. But he knew he saw them. Even if nobody else did. They were real.

NOT ENOUGH PROOF

Back at school, Leo faced off. It was Adam, Manuel, and Angelo. Again. A bunch of students were gathered around. They wanted to see Leo get it.

"You were right," Leo said. "There aren't any zombies. Here. Or anywhere. I lied. You can hit me now, Adam."

Leo closed his eyes. He clenched his fists. And he waited to get punched. He knew he was going down. Then it would be over. It

would be bad. But not as bad as Friday. The
night filled with zombies.

SHIVERING

JUST THINKING
ABOUT IT

After a few seconds, Leo opened his eyes.

"It's no fun when you're telling the
truth," Adam said. "Just stop lying all the
time. Okay?"

Leo nodded.

Adam turned. Then walked away. Manuel
and Angelo followed.

Leo watched them go. Soon there were
only a few kids standing around.

"Wanna play?" Leo asked.

"Okay." A girl with red hair smiled. Her
name was Rachel.

"Okay." Another kid threw him a ball. His name was Wade.

Leo felt really good. Kids wanted to play with him. He was so happy to have friends. He missed this.

He felt good. He wasn't going to lie anymore.

Leo knew he did not need to tell any more stories.

He had lived through a real one.

And that was enough.